D0488788

FRANKIE'S MAGIC FOOTBALL

BY FRANK LAMPARD

FRANKIE'S MAGIC FOOTBALL

FRANKIE VS THE ROWDY ROMANS
FRANK LAMPARD

LITTLE, BROWN BOOKS FOR YOUNG READERS
www.lbkids.co.uk

LITTLE, BROWN BOOKS FOR YOUNG READERS

First published in Great Britain in 2013 by Little, Brown Books
for Young Readers
Reprinted 2013 (five times), 2014

Copyright © 2013 by Lamps On Productions

The moral right of the author has been asserted.

*All characters and events in this publication, other than those
clearly in the public domain, are fictitious and any resemblance
to real persons, living or dead, is purely coincidental.*

All rights reserved.
No part of this publication may be reproduced, stored in a
retrieval system, or transmitted, in any form or by any means, without
the prior permission in writing of the publisher, nor be otherwise circulated
in any form of binding or cover other than that in which it is published
and without a similar condition including this condition being
imposed on the subsequent purchaser.

A CIP catalogue record for this book
is available from the British Library.

ISBN 978-0-349-00160-9

Typeset in Cantarell by M Rules
Printed and bound in Great Britain by
Clays Ltd, St Ives plc

Papers used by LBYR are from well-managed forests
and other responsible sources.

MIX
Paper from
responsible sources
FSC® C104740

Little, Brown Books for Young Readers
An imprint of
Little, Brown Book Group
100 Victoria Embankment
London EC4Y 0DY

An Hachette UK Company
www.hachette.co.uk

www.lbkids.co.uk

Dedication

To my mum Pat, who encouraged
me to do my homework in between
kicking a ball all around the house, and
is still with me every step of the way.

*Welcome to a fantastic
fantasy league – the greatest
football competition ever held in
this world or any other!*

*You'll need four on a team,
so choose carefully. This is a lot
more serious than a game in the
park. You'll never know who your
next opponents will be, or where
you'll face them.*

*So lace up your boots, players,
and good luck! The whistle's
about to blow!*

The Ref

CHAPTER 1

Frankie pressed the bell beside Charlie's front door.

DING-DONG!

"It must have been a dream," said Louise, who was standing next to him.

"But we all had the *same* dream," said Frankie.

Louise rolled her eyes. "There's no such thing as a magic football," she said. "And even if there were, it wouldn't look like that." She pointed to the ball under Frankie's arm.

He smiled. The ball looked like it had been chewed up and spat out again. Half the leather had peeled away, and it sagged like a used teabag. He'd won it at a funfair from a strange old man, but something very weird had happened when they had played with the ball in the park. A portal into another world had opened up, and they'd found themselves on a wooden galleon, playing football against pirates. Well, three pirates and a talking parrot, which was even weirder.

"We can't have been dreaming," said Frankie. "It was the middle of the day."

He heard the sound of footsteps in the house. Max, Frankie's dog, barked.

"And dogs don't talk, either," said Louise.

Max glanced up. On the pirate ship, he'd been chatting away like one of them. But, back in the real world, it was just his usual barks, whines and growls.

The door opened and Charlie stood there. He was wearing his goalie gloves, as always, and was clutching a slice of toast.

"Sorry, guys, just finishing my breakfast," he said.

Louise laughed. "It might be easier if you took them off," she said, nodding at the gloves.

Charlie shook his head. "No way. The best keepers are . . ."

". . . always ready!" said Louise and Frankie together. They had heard it a million times.

Charlie swallowed the last bit of toast. "Let's go."

Just as he stepped through the

door, his ginger cat, Jinx, slipped out after him. Max leapt into the air, then scurried away, tail between his legs. Jinx purred and narrowed her green eyes.

"It's nothing to be frightened of," said Frankie, scratching Max behind the ears.

Jinx leapt up onto the front wall and arched her back.

"She's just a pussycat," said Louise, running her hand over Jinx's fur.

As the friends set off towards the park, Max seemed to recover, trotting a few metres ahead of them and having a good sniff around.

"It's funny how your dog is so fearless about everything else," said Charlie, "but he's terrified of Jinx."

Frankie shrugged. "I guess we're all scared of something. It doesn't have to make sense. I don't like heights."

"I *hate* spiders," said Louise.

They were silent for a few seconds, then Louise asked, "What are you scared of, Charlie?"

"I don't know," said Charlie, chewing his lip. "Nothing, I guess. No, actually, I do know! I'm scared of . . . not saving goals."

Frankie and Louise burst out laughing.

"That doesn't count!" said Frankie.

"Well, I suppose I'm scared of sharks," said Charlie.

"We're *all* scared of sharks," said Frankie. He shuddered as he remembered walking the plank on the pirate ship, and seeing the shark fins cutting through the waves beneath. "Do you think it was real?" he asked.

Charlie shrugged. "It felt real to me. Has anything else happened with the ball since?"

Frankie shook his head. "Nope." He'd tried playing with it in his garden and even in his bedroom. No more portals had opened up. It was sort of a relief — on the pirate ship, they'd almost ended up marooned on a desert island. But Frankie couldn't help feeling disappointed too. "I've got a theory, though," he said. "Maybe it only works when we're all together."

"Frankie's FC might not be finished yet!" said Louise.

A light drizzle had started by the time they reached the park, so there weren't many people about. Frankie dropped his ball and chipped it into Charlie's gloves.

"Looks like we'll get the pitch

to ourselves," said Charlie, as they made their way to the grass where they played.

"Or not," said Louise, pointing ahead. "Uh oh."

Frankie looked up and his heart sank. His older brother, Kevin, was already there with his mates, Liam, Rob and Matt. Matt was in goal between the two posts. They were kicking around a gleaming new football.

"Woah!" said Charlie. "That's a 'Football Pro Infinity'. They cost loads."

Frankie felt himself blushing. He suddenly wanted to hide his battered old football. "Come on, let's find somewhere else."

But it was too late. His brother blasted a shot past Matt and the ball rolled towards Frankie. He stopped it under his foot.

"Look who it is!" said Kevin. "*Frankenstein* and his loser mates."

Frankie's embarrassment turned to anger. He put up with his brother picking on him, but not his friends. *Time to teach them a lesson*, he thought. "Hi, Kev," he said. "Can we play, too?"

Kevin glanced at his friends as he walked over. "No way," he sneered. "It's not a *children's* game."

He tried to kick the ball from under Frankie's foot, but Frankie rolled it back out of reach.

"Give me the ball, Frankenstein," said Kevin, his face darkening. "Or else."

"Sure," said Frankie. He dribbled

the ball to his brother, then tipped
it through his legs.

"Oi!" said Kevin. "I said, give—"

Frankie wasn't listening. He
passed the ball to Louise. Liam
and Rob were closing in. Louise
dummied to pass back to Frankie
but took the ball around Rob.
Charlie was laughing. "Go, Frankie's
team!" he shouted. Liam was a big
kid, and quick. He ran at Louise,
but she kept her nerve and flicked
the ball over his head. It came to
Frankie, in front of goal.

Matt spread his arms. "You're not
getting past me," he said.

Want a bet? thought Frankie.

"Hey, that's ours!" came Charlie's voice.

Frankie turned, forgetting about shooting. Max was barking, running in circles around Kevin, who was holding their football from the fair.

"*Children* play in the *children's* area," Kevin said. "Now beat it!" He tossed the old ball in the air, then booted it high and far.

Frankie watched his ball fly towards the toddlers' play area.

And then suddenly he was on the ground, as Liam tackled him roughly and took the other ball.

"Great shot, Kev!" called Matt.

He lowered his voice and muttered to Frankie, "Told you that you wouldn't score."

CHAPTER 2

Frankie picked himself up, hanging his head and avoiding his brother's eye as he joined his friends. Together, they trudged off to find their ball.

"Just ignore him," said Louise. "Your brother's only jealous because you're better at football than he is."

"Yeah," said Charlie, grinning.

"He's probably jealous of your ball, too."

Frankie looked at his friend, who was smirking. He couldn't help smiling, too. His ball had cost him fifty pence rather than fifty pounds.

The rain started to fall even harder. Great grey sheets poured from the sky, so it was hard to see very far ahead. Behind them, Frankie could hear Kevin and his mates shouting that they should find somewhere to shelter.

"We'd better go, too," said Frankie. This was turning into a disaster. "Max, go and get the ball."

Max streaked off. Frankie squinted ahead and saw his dog pause for a moment on the edge of the play area. Then he darted towards the sandpit, and leapt over the side.

He vanished with a howl.

"Max!" called Frankie.

"What happened to him?" said Louise, panic in her voice.

Frankie broke into a run. He was soaked to the skin now. He vaulted the fence into the play area and dashed to the sandpit's edge.

The sand had gone, replaced by a pool of swirling colours.

"It's just like the portal from

before," said Charlie, huffing as he caught up.

Frankie nodded slowly. "Max must have fallen through," he mumbled.

"What shall we do?" asked Charlie.

Frankie stared into his friends' faces. Rain had matted their hair and soaked their clothes. "I can't ask you to come with me," he said. "Max is my dog, it's my responsibility."

"We're coming," said Louise. "No question. The best teams always stick together."

"She's right," said Charlie. "Try stopping us."

Frankie's heart surged with relief. *I should never have doubted them.*

He held out both hands, and Louise and Charlie took one each. Whatever waited for them on the other side, they'd face it together. "Ready?" he asked.

Charlie gave a brisk nod and Louise squeezed his hand tighter.

Frankie leapt into the kaleidoscope of colour. Both his friends' hands were wrenched from his. Everything went dark.

The first thing Frankie realised was that he was dry. Dry and warm.

That's a good start, he thought.

"Lou?" he said. "Charlie?"

"I can't see anything," said Louise.

"Me, neither," whimpered Charlie. "And, by the way, I *am* afraid of something – the dark!"

"Don't worry," said Frankie, groping about in the gloom. Metal clanked and echoed. Frankie shuffled forward. More clanking, and he almost tripped.

"I've got chains on my feet and ankles," he said.

The sound of shifting chains seemed to come from all around him.

"Me, too," said Louise.

"Oh, great!" said Charlie.

A low growl rumbled on the air.

"Jinx?" said Charlie.

"That sounded *bigger* than Jinx," said a husky voice that Frankie recognised.

"Is that you, Max?" he said. He felt a wet nose brush his leg.

"Sorry I got you all into this mess," said Max.

"What mess?" said Charlie. "Where *are* we?"

Frankie suddenly heard whistling, and a faint glow appeared in the distance. It grew brighter, until he saw it was the flickering flame of a torch, in the hand of a large man. He also made out thick wooden stakes and iron bars all around them.

"We're in a cage!" he said.

The man holding the torch walked towards the edge of the bars. With him came a draught of smelly air: old feet and rotten onions. Judging by the man's toothless, dirt–and–sweat–smeared face, Frankie guessed he was the source of the stench. He looked a bit like Frankie's next–door neighbour, Mr Pratchett – if Mr Pratchett hadn't been to the dentist for about a hundred years.

"Hey!" said Charlie, rushing to the bars as fast as his chains would allow. "Let us out of here!"

The man sniggered, and another waft of stinkiness almost knocked Frankie off his feet.

"Oh, you'll be out of there soon enough," he said, still tittering to himself. "Your team's up next."

"Our team?" said Frankie. He looked down and realised he was wearing a dirty white tunic and leather sandals. On his chest was the same badge that had appeared when he had faced the pirates. It read *FFC*.

"Frankie's Football Club," he said

to himself. "Guys, we're going to play another match!"

"Hurray!" said Louise. She was wearing a tatty tunic too, with a cape behind it.

"Let's hope we're not getting fed to the sharks at the end," said Charlie.

Their jailer frowned. "No

sharks today," he hissed. "They're not flooding the arena until next week."

Arena? thought Frankie. *Where are we?* He knew of someone who could tell him. "Can we speak to the Ref?" he asked.

The jailer bashed the cage bars with his stick. "Who's this 'Ref' then?" he snarled. "One of the other gladiators?"

"Gladiators?" said Louise. She gripped Frankie's shoulder. "We must be in Ancient Rome!"

The jailer shook his head. "You're a funny bunch, aren't you? We just call it Rome."

An enormous roar shook Frankie to his bones.

"That sounded *a lot* bigger than Jinx," said Max.

The jailer smiled. "That'll be Ferox. Better pray he's not hungry. Ha! What am I saying? Ferox is *always* hungry."

Charlie's eyes were like saucers.

"You ready?" said the jailer, opening the door of the cage.

"No!" chorused Frankie and his friends.

CHAPTER 3

The jailer led them along a low corridor. They shuffled and rattled along in their chains. Torchlight threw long shadows on the walls. Every few steps, they passed alcoves that led to other cells. In the gloom, Frankie made out figures crouched in their cages: just whites of eyes,

with the occasional glint of steel —
armour and blades. The air smelled
of stale sweat and fear.

*They must be the other
gladiators*, he thought. *They don't
look much like football players!*

From somewhere above came
the hum of voices: hundreds, maybe
thousands of them. Frankie felt
a bead of sweat trickle down his
cheek. His heart was thumping in
his chest.

The jailer led them around
several corners, and then up a long
ramp towards a towering wooden
gate.

"Perhaps we should go back

to that nice warm cell," muttered Max.

The jailer raised his stick and banged three times on the wooden gate. He turned to Frankie and his friends. "Too late for that now," he said. "Your audience awaits!"

A rhythmic thumping began on the other side of the gate. Frankie realised the crowd were stamping their feet in unison.

As the jailer walked between them, unlocking the chains at their ankles, the pounding grew louder, and faster and faster, until it felt as if the walls were shaking.

"We'll be all right," Frankie said to the others.

The jailer grinned. "They all say that."

With a groan of hinges, the gates swung outwards.

Frankie was blinded and deafened at once. Daylight flooded the rampway, and the roar of voices created a wall of sound. He rocked back on his heels, but the jailer gave him a shove in the back.

"Wow!" said Louise.

Frankie stumbled through the gates. Blinking into the glare, he gasped. Steep tiers of seats rose up on every side, with great

stone arches built one on top of
the other. The stands were full to
bursting with what must have been
thirty thousand people, all wearing
tunics, or togas of every colour,
or dresses draped in many folds.
Their eyes bore into him. Frankie
turned slowly. He and his friends
were standing on one side of an
enormous circular pitch, but instead
of grass on the ground, there was
a thin layer of sand over hard-
packed earth. He felt tiny, as if he
was standing in the centre circle at
Wembley on Cup Final day.

"This is the Colosseum!" said
Louise. "We learnt about it at school.

It's one of the largest buildings in Ancient Rome, built in the first century for gladiatorial contests . . ."

"Not football matches?" said Charlie.

"No," said Frankie, with a giant gulp. "Fights to the death."

"Oh," said Max. "And I was just hoping for a run in the park."

From somewhere in the arena, a drum beat slowly. Two servants with bare chests began to close the gates behind them, and the jailer gave them a little wave.

"See you soon!" called Charlie bravely.

"I doubt it," said the jailer. Then

the doors slammed closed and he was gone.

The drums sped up, hammering more quickly. Frankie noticed that the eyes of the crowd had all shifted in one direction. He followed them with his own and saw a man standing far across the arena from them. He wore black and had something hung around his neck: some sort of necklace. "Guys!" Frankie said. "Look!"

The black-clad man made his way to a raised podium as the drumbeat quickened to a crescendo. As he lowered himself into a throne-like seat, the drums stopped dead.

"That's not right," said Louise, frowning. "That's where the emperor should sit. But he wore purple, not black."

Frankie suddenly realised what the necklace was — a whistle. And now he recognised the face, too. "It's not the emperor," he said. "It's the Ref!"

"Welcome, challengers!" bellowed a bald man beside the Ref. "State your team name!"

Frankie cleared his throat. He wasn't going to let his fear get the better of him. "Frankie's FC!" he called.

Thousands of boos rolled

from the stands. The noise was incredible – shouts and screams and hisses.

"We're definitely the away team," said Louise nervously.

The Ref reached down and picked something round off a stand in front of him. He lifted it above his head.

"The ball!" said Frankie. "*Our* ball!"

The Ref hurled the ball into the arena. It rolled to a stop right in the centre.

"Where's the goal?" Charlie shouted.

Two pairs of servants appeared at opposite sides of the pitch.

They lifted two pairs of posts into position, facing each other.

"This should be a doddle," said Max, scampering towards the ball. "The other side hasn't even shown up!" Suddenly a trumpet blared, and Max froze.

"Welcome the Rowdy Romans!" cried the bald herald at the Ref's side.

The gates opposite Frankie and his team burst open in a cloud of sand and dust, and two figures entered. They couldn't have been more different. One was a skinny, bare-chested man, who must have weighed about the same as Frankie.

He wore a helmet, a studded belt and a kind of leather skirt. Clutching a long, three-pronged trident in one hand, he dragged a net in the other.

Next to him stood a giant, a man-mountain over seven feet tall. His helmet was so big it looked like he was wearing a small dustbin on his head, while his chest and arms were clad in thick, dented armour. He carried a deadly looking club.

"Beware Snatcher and Brutus!" yelled the herald. The crowd cheered. "And their leader . . ." continued the announcer, "Captain Lasher!"

The cries went wild as a horse
charged into the arena, scattering
the servants who'd opened the
gates. It drew an open-topped
chariot in which stood a tall woman
wearing tight-fitting leather armour
and cracking a whip in the air. At
the centre of the arena, she pulled

back sharply on the reins and the chariot skidded to a halt. Behind it, the dust settled.

Captain Lasher turned her steely gaze on Frankie and his team, and smiled. "This shouldn't take long," she said.

CHAPTER 4

"We're toast," said Charlie. "Even if we *have* got one more player than they do."

"They're not that scary," said Louise, throwing a glance towards Brutus. "Remember when we played St Dunstan's School? They had a big defender, too."

He didn't have a club, though, thought Frankie.

The Ref blew his whistle and the herald turned over a large egg-timer filled with sand. "Let battle commence!"

Frankie and his teammates ran for the ball. At the same time, Captain Lasher sent her horse forward with a whip-crack. She also appeared to be winding something at waist-height with her other hand, balancing perfectly in the chariot.

What's she up to? Frankie wondered

THWANG!

Frankie saw something spinning by the side of her chariot, and realised too late what it was.

Slingshot!

A ball of wood the size of his head hurtled towards him. Just before it hit, a shape leapt to his side. Charlie caught the ball on his gloves and it thumped into the sand.

"Thanks!" said Frankie.

THWANG!

Another ball shot out, this time heading straight for Max. The little dog froze.

Charlie dived across to stop the shot, catching it in mid-air.

"Great save," called Max. "I was almost a fur pancake!"

"Surely that's a foul!" said Louise.

Captain Lasher drew up her chariot alongside the football and scooped it up in one hand.

"*And* that!" said Louise. "Handball!"

Frankie looked up hopefully at the Ref, but he was sitting down now, hardly paying attention: one servant was fanning him with a huge plume of peacock feathers; another was offering him a goblet and a platter of grapes.

Captain Lasher cackled. "Silly

girl! There aren't any rules in the Colosseum!" She tugged hard on the reins and began steering her chariot towards the goal.

Frankie knew he couldn't catch a galloping horse. His eyes landed on one of the wooden balls. Without stopping to think, he grabbed it, spun around and hurled it with a grunt. *If I can just distract her . . .*

The wooden ball landed right in the chariot's path. Captain Lasher pulled hard at the reins to avoid it, and the chariot tipped as one wheel left the ground. "Argh!" she cried, as it toppled sideways.

Frankie winced as she spilled out

into the dust. The football rolled loose and Louise was quickly on it.

Covered in dust, Captain Lasher climbed to her feet and began to right her fallen chariot. Frankie was glad she wasn't hurt. "You won't get away with this!" she yelled.

But the crash had broken her slingshot to bits. *Now to win the game.* "Louise! Go!" Frankie said, pointing to the goal. His friend turned and began to run. But Brutus was now lumbering into her path.

"On the wing!" called Max. "Pass it! Pass it!"

Louise looked up, saw Max and

made to pass. But then a net fell silently yet accurately over her head, and her feet tangled up. She fell headlong in a heap.

"Gotcha!" said Snatcher, the gladiator with the net. He spiked the ball with his trident and held it aloft.

"Give me ball!" said Brutus.

"I want to score," said Snatcher.

Brutus raised his club. "You score always. Goal-hogger. My turn."

Snatcher's face twisted in disgust, but he flung the ball towards the massive armoured gladiator.

Frankie saw his chance as

the ball flew through the air. He sprinted to get there first. Brutus saw him coming and swung his club. Frankie dodged before it cracked his skull and took the ball, leaving Brutus spinning around dizzily.

A few metres away, Max was busy trying to tug the net off Louise. Charlie was making his way towards their goal, just in case he had to make a save. *It's up to me*, thought Frankie.

Brutus now raised the club and charged like a bull. "Me squash boy!"

You're too slow! Frankie

thought, *just like the defender at St Dunstan's.* But, just then, out of the corner of his eye, he noticed with a shock that Snatcher was approaching from the other direction, stabbing the air with his trident.

Time for a new tactic.

Frankie lifted his foot and blasted the ball at Brutus. It struck his leg, making him stumble.

The crowd sucked in a breath as one: "OOOH!"

The ball bounced back to Frankie, and he took aim and fired again. This time, the ball slammed into Snatcher's helmet, spinning it

around on his head so he couldn't
see.

"AAAH!" gasped the spectators.

Brutus had righted himself and
was now swinging his club wildly,
getting closer still. Frankie booted
the ball hard and this time it hit the
club, sending it flying out of the
gladiator's hand.

The crowd didn't say anything, which surprised Frankie. Then he turned and saw why.

Captain Lasher was in her chariot again. And she was thundering straight towards him.

CHAPTER 5

Captain Lasher was twirling her whip over her head, her eyes gleaming with hatred. The horse snorted wildly. The ground shook under Frankie's feet.

"Run!" yelled Lou.

But Frankie knew that if he turned and ran the chariot would easily catch him. He held his nerve.

"Crush him like a grape!" cried Snatcher. Frankie saw him hopping up and down gleefully.

Sand sprayed up from under the horse's hooves and from the churning wheels of the chariot.

"Grind his bones!" growled Brutus.

When Frankie was close enough to see the intricate patterns on Captain Lasher's armour, he bent his legs and dived sideways. He felt the hot breath of the horse and a rush of air as the chariot shot past.

Frankie rolled over and found his feet again as he coughed and blinked in a huge cloud of dust. Squinting, he tried desperately to see out of it.

"Did I get him?" Captain Lasher was shouting. "Did I squash the boy?"

"Where's Frankie?" yelled Charlie. "Frankie!"

"I'm here!" called Frankie, glancing about. "Where's the ball?"

"I see it!" barked Max. The little dog dashed into a patch of swirling sand, just as Snatcher rushed in from the other side.

"*Grrrr!*"

"Ouch!"

"That's mine!"

"Get off me, you little . . ."

"Foul!"

"That's my leg!"

Max scampered out from the cloud with the ball in his teeth. As the dust settled, Frankie saw Snatcher squirming on the ground, tangled in his own net.

"You fool!" screamed Captain Lasher.

Max dropped the ball between his paws and passed it to Louise. The chariot turned and bore down on her. Louise chipped the ball over the horse and it

dropped to Frankie. There was
nothing between him and the
goal.

Nothing other than seven feet of
muscles and armour: Brutus.

"Come, boy!" Brutus said. "You
not get past me now." He spread
his trunk-like legs and tossed
his helmet aside. He was bald
on top, and his head looked like
a misshapen potato, but even
dirtier. He didn't seem to have a
neck at all.

Frankie simply dribbled the ball
between his legs.

"Nutmegged him!" shouted
Charlie.

Frankie was clear on goal. *Just hold your nerve.*

Ten metres out, he lifted his foot to shoot.

SPLAT!

Something wet hit Frankie's cheek and he stumbled. The ball rolled away.

Frankie felt his face. *Urgh!* It was slimy. Then his eye fell on a rotten apple on the ground.

SPLAM!

A mouldy cabbage landed at his feet and the spectators jeered.

"What's going on?" Frankie muttered. As he looked up, half a loaf of mouldy bread sailed through the air towards his head.

A gloved hand batted it away.
"Looks like the home crowd is
turning against us," said Charlie.
"Look out!"

He reached past Frankie's
face and caught a floppy carrot.
Now things began to rain down
from every side: rotten fruit and
vegetables; stinky fish-heads;
sandals; even a pottery flask that
smashed into shards, showering
their legs with sharp bits. Frankie
skipped from side to side, ducking
and jumping, while Charlie did his
best to stop as many missiles as
possible. But there were too many
even for him and soon the whole

goalmouth was filled with rubbish
and old food.

Frankie and Charlie backed off
towards the centre, leaving the ball.
Only Max braved the downpour, to
snatch up what looked like a large
bone.

A piercing whistle cut through
the crowd's boos and all eyes went

to the Ref. Frankie saw that the sand in the timer had run out.

The Ref whispered to the herald, who then rose to face the arena. "Friends, Romans, boys and girls!" he proclaimed. "Listen up! Normal time has ended, and the Ref's bottom is getting tired. The game will be decided by sudden death. The next team to score will be the victor."

"I wonder what happens to the losers," said Charlie.

"You'll be back in the dungeon for a long time," said Captain Lasher.

"But we've got school on

Monday," said Louise. "I've been revising for a maths test."

"Well, you can count the rats down there," came Captain Lasher's reply.

As Frankie's teammates lined up alongside him, servants cleared away the debris from the goalmouth. Brutus dragged Snatcher to his feet and they took their places behind their leader's chariot.

Frankie realised for the first time that he was afraid. Not of being run over by a chariot, skewered by a trident, or bear-hugged by a giant. Scared of failing his friends.

"I'm sorry I brought us here," he said.

"It's not your fault," said Charlie. "It was Max who jumped into the portal."

Max looked up from his bone, ears drooping. "Don't blame me – I was just trying to get the ball. I'm a dog. I fetch."

"It's no one's fault," said Louise. "And we're *not* going to lose."

"It's not fair," grumbled Snatcher. "They've got one more player than us."

Captain Lasher grinned. "Not for long." She cracked her whip and the ground in front of her chariot opened up.

"A trapdoor!" said Charlie.
"Cool!"

The crowd began mumbling a word, but Frankie couldn't hear what it was. As the chant got louder, he realised they were saying "Ferox! Ferox! Ferox!"

From the trapdoor in the arena floor emerged a huge, shaggy head of tawny fur.

"Er . . . not cool," said Louise.

A lion padded into the arena and the crowd went wild.

CHAPTER 6

The lion looked around, and his black eyes settled on Frankie.

"I guess that's Ferox," said Charlie with a gulp.

Opening his mouth like a red chasm, the lion roared. Frankie saw gleaming white canines as long as his fingers. *Slingshots, whips,*

hooves, nets, clubs and tridents,
thought Frankie. *And now teeth
and claws. Can this match get any
tougher?*

The whistle blew.

Ferox prowled forward and stood
over the ball.

"Anyone fancy tackling him?"
asked Frankie hopefully.

Louise and Charlie shook their
heads.

Ferox began to walk slowly
towards their goal, with the ball
under his paws.

We need a distraction, thought
Frankie. He turned to Max. "Better
give me that bone, Max," he said.

"No way!" said the dog. "It's mine. Finder's keepers!"

"If you don't hand it over," said Louise, "it might be all you have to eat for a long time. I don't think the catering in the dungeons is five star."

Max grumbled, but tossed the bone to Frankie.

Frankie picked it up. "Hey, Ferox!" he called, holding the bone aloft. The lion turned his head and sniffed. "I've got a treat for you!"

Ferox left the ball and ran towards Frankie, who hurled the bone back over his head and watched the lion sprint after it.

Brutus reached the ball at the same moment as Louise. She bounced off the mountain of muscle and landed on her backside.

"Pass it!" called Snatcher.

Brutus set off towards the goal in lumbering strides.

"To me! To me!" shrieked Captain Lasher.

Brutus didn't even look up from the ball.

He wants the glory for himself, thought Frankie. *We'll see about that.*

"Charlie, get out on the wing," he said, dashing after Brutus. "Hey, big guy!" he shouted.

Brutus looked up, grimaced and swung his club. Frankie dropped into a slide, skidding beneath the club, and managed to get his foot to the ball. He looked for Charlie and saw him moving towards the goal. Frankie passed the ball and watched it fly straight and true to his friend.

"Great pass!" yelled Louise. "Shoot, Charlie!"

Charlie managed to control the ball. He slammed it goalwards.

Frankie raised his arms to cheer . . .

SMACK!

The ball stopped dead as three

metal prongs stabbed it into the ground.

"It's not over yet!" Snatcher cried. As Charlie chased after the ball, the gladiator swished his net across the ground, flicking sand into Charlie's face.

"Argh!" Charlie said. "I can't see!" He staggered back and forth, trying to wipe the sand out of his eyes.

"Take your gloves off!" shouted Louise.

She might as well tell Max to take off his fur, thought Frankie, turning as he heard pounding hooves and rattling wheels.

Captain Lasher was heading for the spiked ball, and Charlie stood right in her path, stumbling blindly. Frankie started running towards his friend.

"Move left!" yelled Louise.

Charlie sidestepped.

"No, my left!" she cried. "Your right."

Charlie went the other way.

Captain Lasher was closing on him. "He's mine!" she said.

Snatcher was twirling his net, ready to throw it over Charlie's head. "No, he's mine!"

A plan came to Frankie's mind. "Stand your ground, Charlie. Get

ready!" He put on an extra burst of
speed.

"I'm . . . I'm always ready!" said his
friend.

Frankie reached Charlie a
split second before the chariot.
Snatcher's net fell like a shadow
overhead. He bundled into his
friend, bowling him out of the way
like a skittle.

"Out of the way!" screamed
Captain Lasher.

"Stop!" yelped Snatcher.

Frankie and Charlie landed in a
heap. Looking back, Frankie saw
Snatcher being dragged along
behind the chariot, his net tangled

in it wheels. Captain Lasher was hanging onto her reins as the horse careered madly around the arena.

"Dunderheads!" roared Brutus. "You let th—argh!" He didn't finish his sentence as he was sent spinning by the chariot as it charged past him.

Louise tugged the trident free of the ball. "Let's finish this," she said.

But as they turned towards the goal, something very big, very hairy and very fierce filled the space between them and the goalposts. It ran its tongue down one of its tusk-like teeth. "You forgot about me, didn't you?" Ferox said.

Charlie, finally able to see again, joined Frankie and Louise. "Any more bright ideas? I don't fancy trying to dribble the ball around those claws."

Frankie was about to volunteer when Max trotted up and nosed the ball. "Well, if none of you are brave enough . . ."

As he walked towards the goal, Ferox the lion strode out to meet him.

"I don't want to look," said Charlie.

When they were a couple of metres apart, Ferox roared, blasting Max's fur like a hurricane.

Max sat back on his haunches, his front paws tucked under the ball.

Frankie began to understand what he was up to – they'd practised this trick in his back garden last Sunday.

"Aren't you scared?" asked Ferox.

"Why would I be scared?" growled Max.

"Because I'm a lion," said Ferox. "And you're a puny little dog. I wouldn't even have to chew."

Frankie saw Max quiver and edged forward.

"I know that," said Max. "But the thing is . . ."

"Yes?" growled Ferox, drool spilling from his lips.

"Thing is," said Max, "I'm just causing a distraction."

Max suddenly sprang up, flicking the ball high in the air. Ferox jerked his body to follows its arcing path . . .

. . . right to Frankie . . .

. . . who lifted his right foot, twisted his hips and connected sweetly.

The volley flew between the posts.

CHAPTER 7

Frankie's teammates piled on top of him.

"SUPERGOOAAALLL!" shouted Louise.

"Even I would have struggled to stop that," admitted Charlie.

"Yeah, not bad," said Max. "I'd lick your face, but it looks sort of dirty."

Frankie patted his head. "You're the Man of the Match," he said. "The way you stood up to that lion was incredible."

Max lifted his shoulders in a doggy shrug. "It was nothing. Like Lou said, 'Just a pussycat'."

Frankie realised the crowd had gone completely silent. He let his eyes sweep over the thousands of unsmiling faces. *They weren't expecting us to win* . . .

"Ouch! Argh! No!"

On the other side of the arena, Captain Lasher was giving Brutus and Snatcher a taste of her whip.

"You're pathetic!" she raged.
"I'd be better substituting you for
statues, for all the good you did.
Call that footwork, Brutus? Call
that marking, Snatcher?"

Charlie grabbed the ball out of
the net and held it aloft for the Ref
to see.

"The game's over!" he cried.
"Now let us go."

The Ref looked down on them,
eyes fierce, but it was the herald
who spoke, looking down his nose
at them.

"The game is not over until the
Referee decides," he said. "Thumbs
up, you may leave. Thumbs down,

it's back in the dungeons to fight another day."

The Referee held out his arms, thumbs pointed sideways.

"Dungeons!" called one of the spectators.

"Feed them to Ferox!" called another.

The Ref's thumbs began to turn downwards.

"This isn't fair!" said Louise. "We won fair and square."

More people were crying out: "Ferox! Ferox!"

"I don't think the rules are quite the same here," said Frankie. As the shouts grew louder, his hopes began to fade. "I'm sorry, guys," he said. "I tried—"

"Frankie, listen!" said Charlie, a smile starting to spread over his face.

Frankie stopped talking. Louise was grinning too, and he realised why. The crowd had stopped shouting the lion's name. They were chanting something else.

"FRAN-*KIE*! FRAN-*KIE*! FRAN-*KIE*!"

Frankie glanced at the Ref. His thumbs turned upwards and the cheers shook the arena. Pride swelled in his chest.

"Release them!" cried the herald. "The winners are Frankie's FC."

Two servants rushed to the
main gate and drew back its heavy
bolts.

As the doors opened, an
incredible sight met their eyes.
Frankie saw gleaming temples
clad in colourful stone, soaring
arches and stately colonnades. Hills

covered in grand villas rose in the distance.

"Ancient Rome!" gasped Louise.

"Stop that lion!" bellowed the herald.

Before the servants could move, Ferox had slipped through the open gate.

"At least one of their team escaped the dungeon," said Charlie.

"Let's go home," said Max, scampering ahead.

Frankie followed him, waving to the crowd. But doubts were growing in the back of his mind. What if they couldn't get home?

"Where'd Max go?" asked Charlie, slightly ahead. "He was here a moment ago."

Then he vanished too.

As Frankie stepped through the gates, sunlight blinded him. When he opened his eyes, he was standing ankle-deep in the sandpit, back in the park.

Wisps of spent cloud hung in the sky and water dripped from the trees. The others hopped out of the wet sand.

"Hey, where've you been?" It was Kevin's voice.

Max barked and Frankie spun around. His brother was walking

towards them, ball in hand and mates in tow.

"We . . . we were just playing football," said Frankie.

"In a sandpit?" said Kevin, frowning.

"Yes!" said Charlie and Louise together.

Kevin narrowed his eyes suspiciously. "Well, anyway, listen. We thought we'd give you a game anyway, now the rain's stopped."

"A game?" said Frankie.

Kevin waved his ball. "Y'know, *football*, Frankenstein. Unless you're scared?"

Frankie grinned and looked at the

others. "Scared? No, we don't scare very easily."

As Kevin led them back to the pitch, he looked Frankie up and down. "Why aren't you soaked? It was bucketing down a minute ago."

"Er . . ." Frankie searched for an answer.

"We hid under . . . um, the slide," said Louise.

At the dinner table that evening, Kevin was sulking.

"What's got into you?" asked Frankie's mum. "You've got a face like you sucked a lemon."

"Nothing," grumbled Kev.

He lost 3–1 to a group of kids, thought Frankie, laying his knife and fork aside. They'd had his favourite: fish and chips. Max was sitting beside his chair looking up hopefully for scraps.

Frankie's dad came in with a cup of tea and sat down. "Well, here's something to cheer you up," he said. "I just heard on the radio that there's a lion on the loose in town." He chuckled, obviously not taking it seriously.

Frankie felt blood rushing to his face. *It can't be* . . .

"That's stupid," said Kev, pushing some mushy peas around his plate.

His dad took a sip from his mug. "Apparently they've had to get the zookeeper out to track it down," he said. "Big thing it is, with a huge mane."

Frankie managed to recover, and glanced down at Max. "It's probably just a big pussycat," he said, with a grin.

Acknowledgements

Many thanks to everyone at
Little, Brown Book Group; Neil
Blair, Zoe King, Daniel Teweles
and all at The Blair Partnership;
Mike Jackson for bringing my
characters to life; special thanks
to Michael Ford for all his wisdom
and patience; and to Steve
Kutner for being a great friend

and for all his help and guidance not just with this book but with everything.

Have you had a chance to check out frankiesmagicfootball.com?

There are activities, news and videos featuring Frank Lampard!

Turn the page for a sneak peek at one of the fun things you can download . . .

Help Frankie and his friends through the maze to find their magic football!